Beautiful Minds
Publishing

Revised edition published by Beautiful Minds Publishing 2021

ISBN: 978-0-9974645-7-3
Library of Congress Cataloging-in-Publication Data is on file.
Printed in the United States of America

This book is dedicated to my son, Daylen Robinson.
You are the best thing that's ever happened to me.
I am so proud to be your mom.
You influenced me to write King, Me.
Always remember, you are greatness!
Anything you want to be, you can be!
I love you!

KiNG, Me

**By
Anece Rochell**

**Illustrated by
Audeva Joseph**

I am a prince,
that will grow
into a king.

Even though I'm young,
I am destined for great things.

I am bright. I am kind,
I see the good in me.
I am capable of being
anything I want to be.

4

I can be a leader, confident and strong.
I will keep my head towards the sky
and ascend to my throne.

Royalty flows through my veins and that part of me will always remain.

I love who I am,
self-love is the key.

Young kings also need
to have high self-esteem.

7

I look in the mirror,
standing tall and proud, saying,
"I see greatness in you child!"

I AM GREATNESS

My dark skin and kinky hair are the creator's gift, it makes me unique and I embrace it.

I am blessed, that I know.
I will continue to evolve, I will grow.

From a boy to a man,
from a prince to a king,
I can conquer the world.
I am ready for anything!

King Me, yes that's me,
and every day I wake up,
that's what I'll strive to be.

The End

Words to know

Ascend   : to rise up

Confident   : a feeling of one's power

Conquer   : overcome and take control of

Destined   : a person's future developing as though according to plan

Embrace   : to accept something

Evolve   : to develop/grow into something better than before

Greatness : the quality of being great

King   : a male ruler/leader

Leader   : a person who leads or commands a group

Royalty   : having the status of a king or queen

Strive   : make great efforts to achieve or obtain something

Umoja   : swahili word for unity

Unique   : unlike anything else

Unity   : to join together as a whole

Introducing
THE UMOJA SQUAD

Ni'Tara

Na'Tasha

Niyah

Daylen

Aaron